For Emma Blackburn

S. M.

For Amelia

R. A.

First U.S. edition 2016

Library of Congress Catalog Card Number 2015936120
ISBN 978-0-7636-8180-7

15 16 17 18 19 20 TLF 10 9 8 7 6 5 4 3 2 1

Printed in Dongguan, Guangdong, China

This book was typeset in Tempus Sans SC ITC.
The illustrations were done in mixed media.

TEMPLAR BOOKS

an imprint of
Candlewick Press
99 Dover Street
Somerville, Massachusetts 02144
www.candlewick.com

WHOOPS!

templar books
an imprint of Candlewick Press

This is the cat
who didn't know how
to sound like a cat.
She couldn't say "meow."

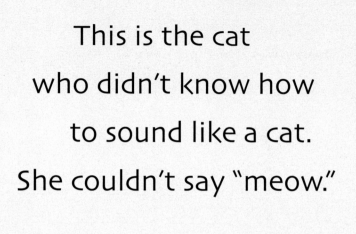

This is the dog
who couldn't bowwow.
He couldn't say "woof."
He didn't know how.

This is the mouse
who tried to speak.
She opened her mouth
but she couldn't say
"squeak."

"Find the old lady in the tumbledown house,"
said the owl to the cat and the dog and the mouse.

"She'll have a spell
to make you all well."

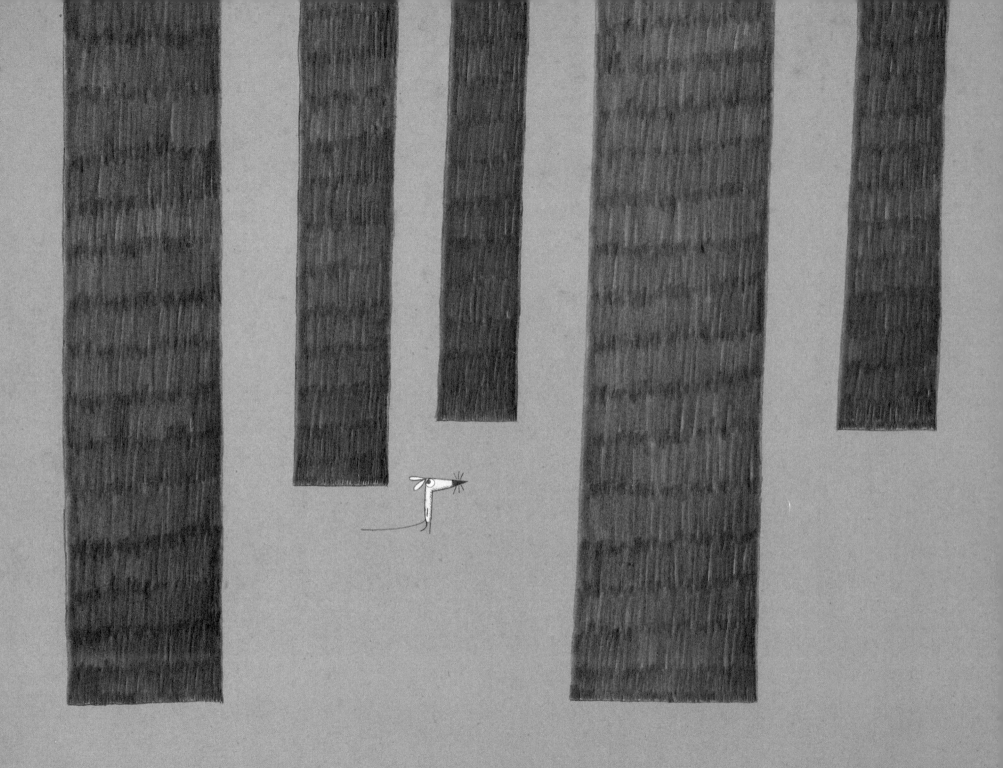

So they went down the lane, and they went through a wood.

The mouse would have squeaked, if only she could.

At the heart of the wood was the tumbledown house.

So in went the cat and the dog and the mouse.

The little old lady, on seeing the three,

said, "I've heard of your problem.

Oh, yes. Goodness me!

Let me find you a spell

to make you all well."

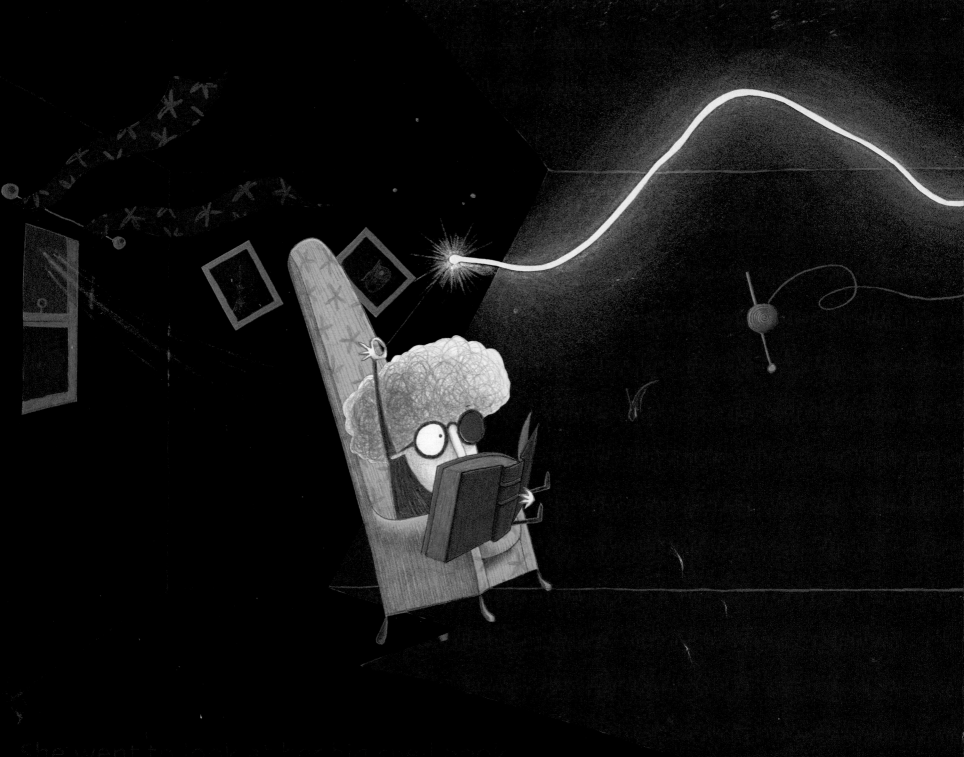

She went to look at her big spell book.
She cast a spell and the window shook.

The wind blew it,

and the rain came down.

Then the tumbledown house

turned around and around.

And the cat said, **CLUCK!**

And the dog said, **QUACK!**

And the mouse (in a shoe) said, **COCK-A-DOODLE-DOO!**

And the little old lady said,

"Oh, silly me!
Let's try page three.
That could be the spell
to make you all well."

She went to look at her big spell book.
She cast a spell, and the whole house shook.

There was a
FLASH!
and a CRASH!
and a rumbling sound.

Then the tumbledown house
turned around and around.

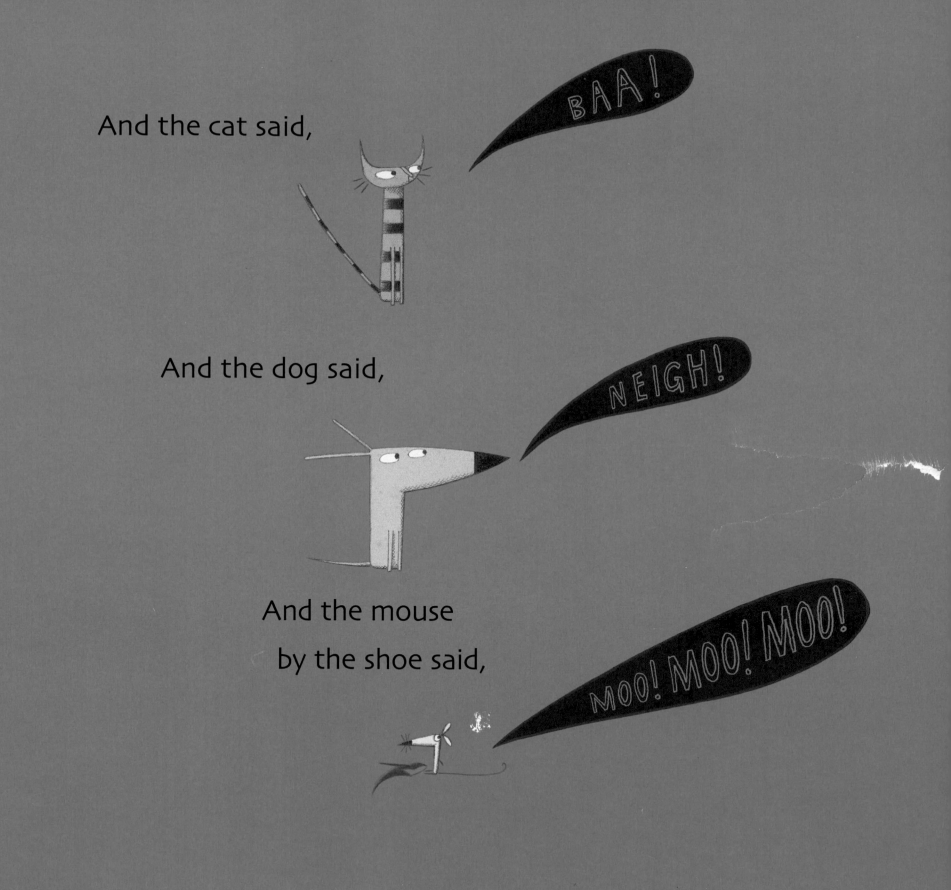

And the little old lady said,

"Oh, good heaven!
Shall we try page seven?
That should be the spell
to make you all well."

She went to look at her big spell book.

She cast a spell, and the whole house shook.

There was a
BANG!
and a CLANG!
and a thundering sound.

Then the tumbledown hoUse
turned around and around.

And the cat said, WOOF!

And the dog said, SQUEAK!

MEOW!

said the mouse
when she tried to speak.

And the little old lady said,

"Oh, not again!
Let's try page ten.
That must be the spell
to make you all well."

She went to look
at her big spell book.

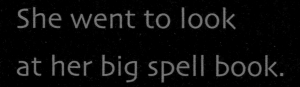

She cast a spell,
and the whole house shook.

There was a sparkle
and a crackle
and a thundering sound.

There was a FLASH!

and a CRASH!

and a rumbling sound.

There was a
BANG!

and a

CLANG!

Then the sky turned brown. The wind blew in,

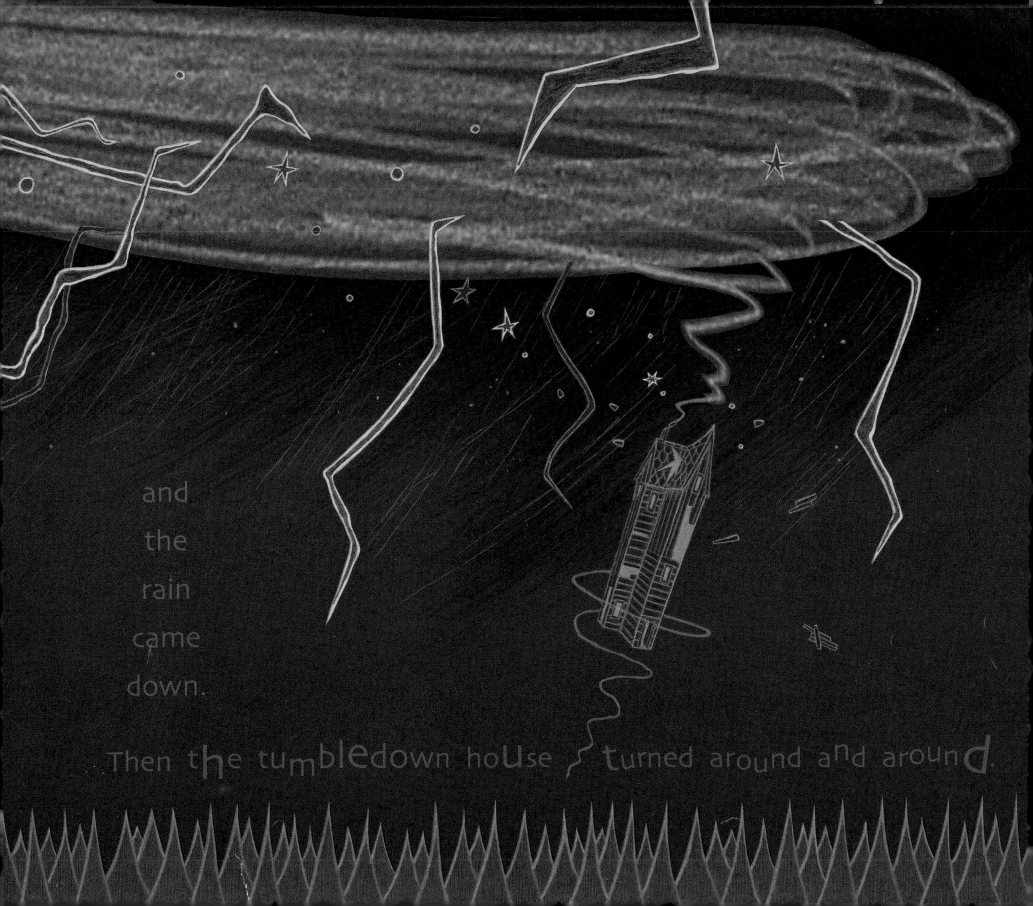

and

the

rain

came

down.

Then the tumbledown house turned around and around.

And the cat said,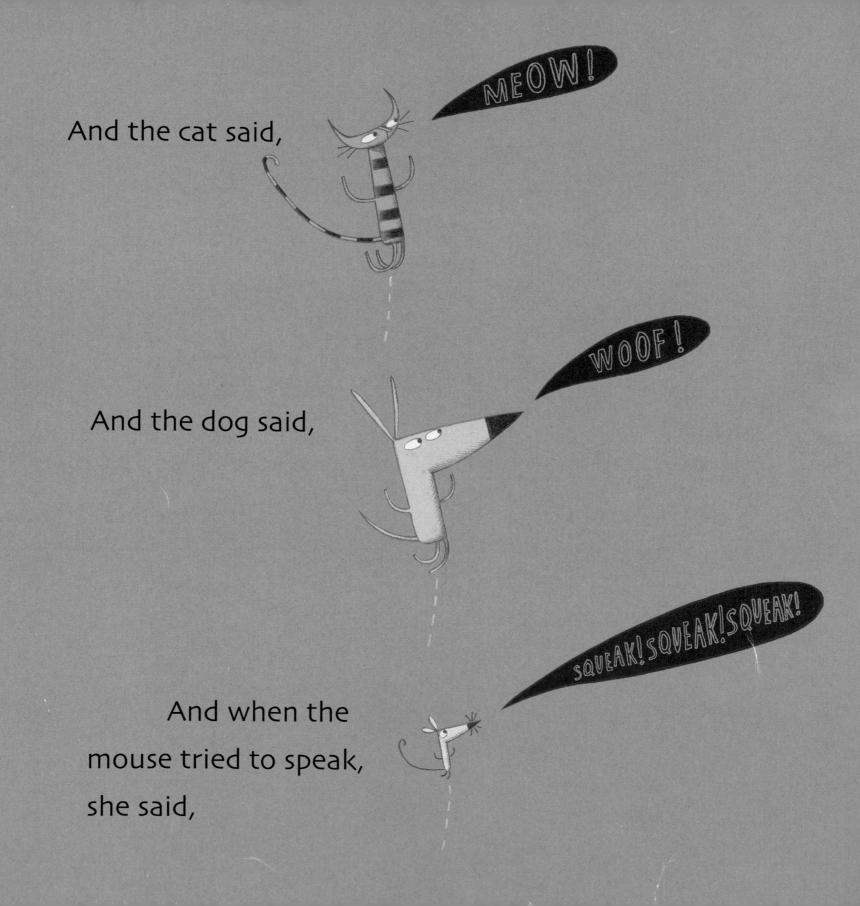

And the dog said,

And when the
mouse tried to speak,
she said,

And the little old lady said,

And the wise old owl,
who was watching from a tree,
looked down with a frown
and he said to the three,

WHOOPS!

Lewis smiled. "Yes. Something was missing. . . .

But now this home is perfect."

As they sat sipping tea and nibbling buns, Joy looked around her new friend's nest. "This home is warm," she said. "This home is cozy."

Joy said, "That sounds lovely. I can bring some cross-top buns."

So Lewis led the way to his house.

Joy laughed. "Oh, my! Now that I get a look at you, I don't find you scary at all." They both chuckled.

"You don't seem scary at all either," said Lewis. "I have an idea, Joy. If you'd like, you could take a break and come to my house for a visit. I have raspberry tea with honey."

"Yes!" Lewis said. He giggled. "That *enormous* creature is me. I'm Lewis. I heard scritching, scratching, and tapping and was afraid it might be an owl, or a cat, or even a bear! I yelled in my biggest voice to scare it away."

"It's . . . it's just me." And out peeked a mouse. A small, gray mouse. "I . . . I . . . My name is Joy."

Lewis blinked. He rubbed his eyes. "Oh," he said. "Um, what are you doing in my tree?"

"*Your* tree? Don't be silly," Joy said. "It's my tree and I'm building a nest for winter. But I keep hearing this . . . this . . . creature bellowing in the night. Oh, it's so very enormous and frightful! Have you heard it?"

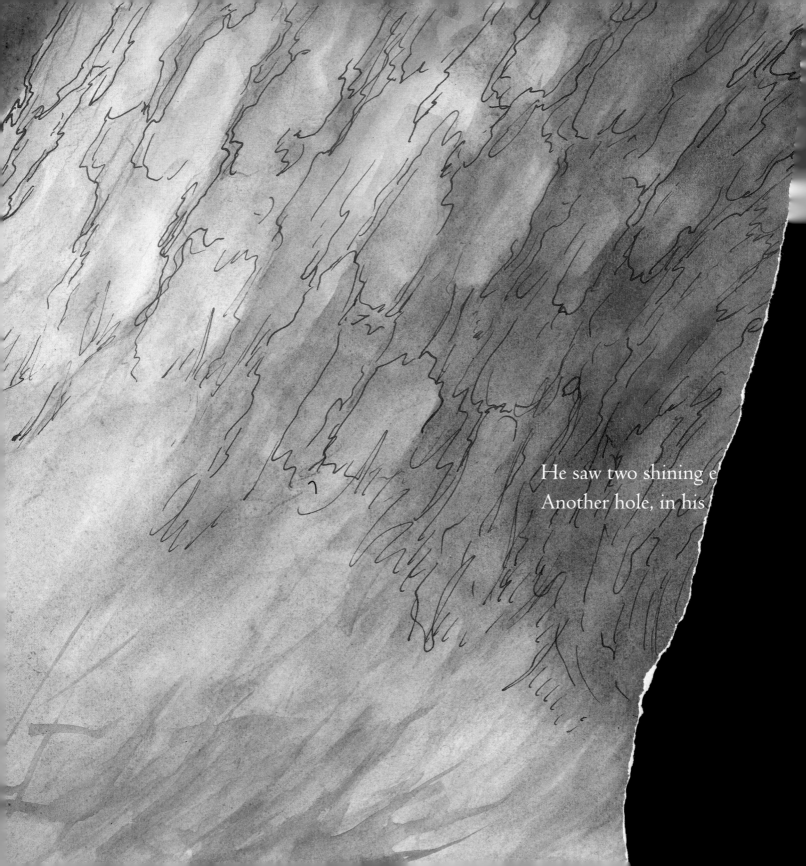

He saw two shining e
Another hole, in his

"WHO IS IT?" cried Lewis.

"WHO GOES THERE?"

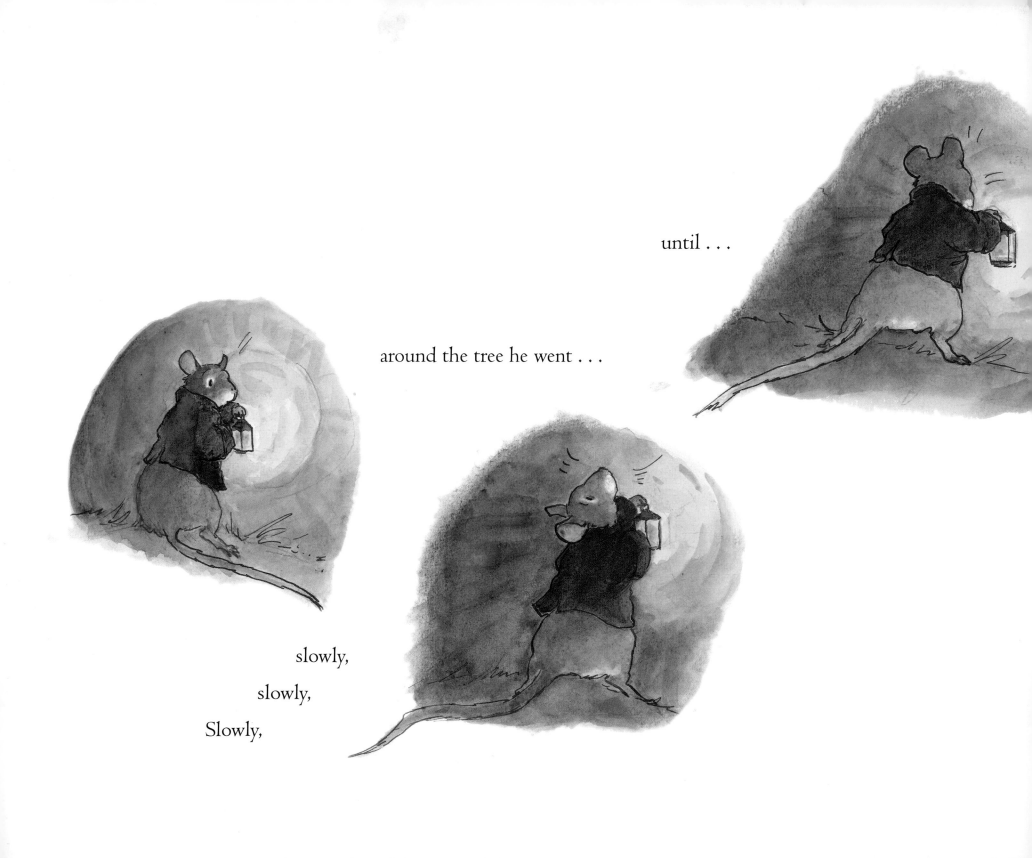

until . . .

around the tree he went . . .

slowly,

slowly,

Slowly,

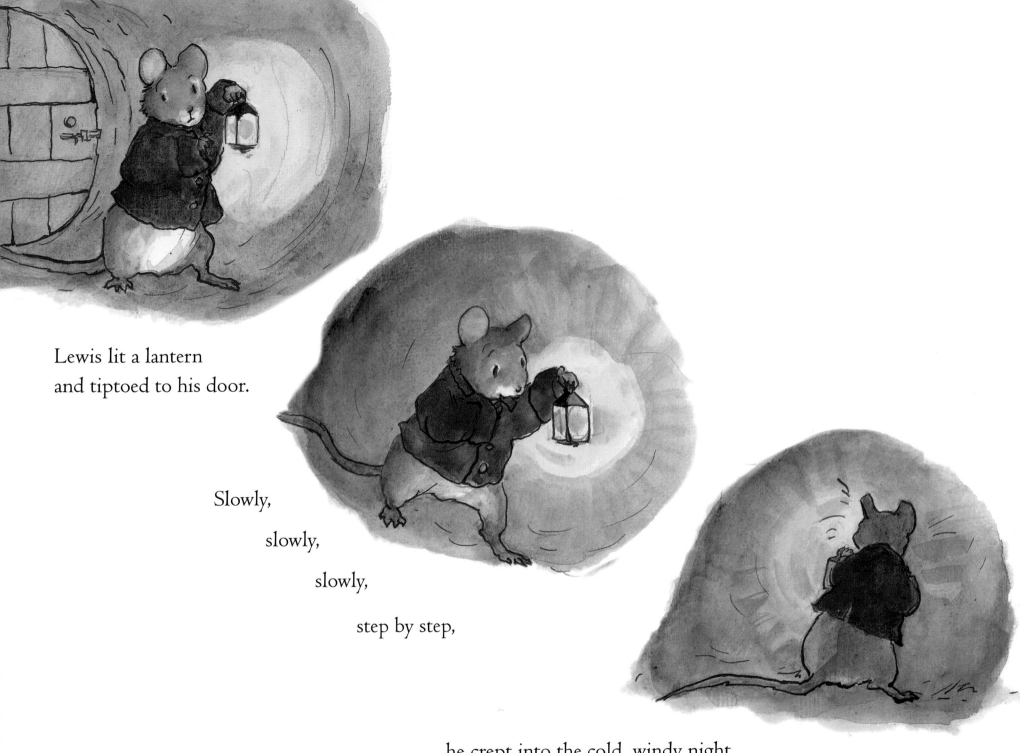

Lewis lit a lantern
and tiptoed to his door.

Slowly,

slowly,

slowly,

step by step,

he crept into the cold, windy night.

Then he whispered,
"Is it a bear? A big, hairy bear?
A big, hairy bear who is
tapping out there?"

"WHO GOES THERE? WHO COULD IT BE?
WHO SCRITCHES AND SCRATCHES AND TAPS AT MY TREE?"

SCRITCH

SCRATCH

TAP

TAP

TAP

"Oh, no!" moaned Lewis.

He gathered all the courage he had left and hollered in his biggest voice yet:

All he heard was the wind.

Since he knew he couldn't possibly sleep, Lewis made a cup of raspberry tea with honey. He tried not to think about the strange noises.

"My nest is warm," said Lewis, "and my nest is cozy. But something is missing. What could it be?"

His thought was rudely interrupted.

Once again he tiptoed to his door and peered into the vast,
dark night and saw . . . nothing.

"Is it a cat? A sneaky old cat?
A sneaky old cat who is
scratching like that?"

SCRITCH

SCRATCH

TAP

TAP TAP

His eyes popped open wide.
He clutched his tail tightly.
What *was* that noise?

SLAM!

He quickly shut his door and skittered to his bed.
"I must try to get some sleep," Lewis decided.
But just as he drifted into a dream . . .

He tiptoed to his door and peeked outside. He peered into the dark and saw . . .
nothing.

"Is it an owl? A great horned owl?
A great horned owl who is out on the prowl?"

Lewis puffed up his chest and roared,

"WHO GOES THERE? WHO COULD IT BE? WHO SCRITCHES AND SCRATCHES AND TAPS AT MY TREE?"

But suddenly, over the wind's song, Lewis heard something he'd never heard before.

SCRITCH
SCRATCH
TAP TAP TAP

Lewis shivered. His whiskers twitched.
What could it be?

"My nest is warm," squeaked Lewis. "My nest is cozy. But something is missing. What could it be?"

Of one thing Lewis was sure: a long, long winter was coming, and coming soon.

"Ah well, I will stay snug inside, nibble seeds, and sing along with the wind."

Lewis Mouse lived all alone in a very small hole at the bottom of a very tall tree. When the first chilly howl of winter bellowed through the trees, Lewis stuffed his nest full of leaves and twigs and grass.

WHO GOES THERE?

Karma Wilson

Illustrated by

Anna Currey

Margaret K. McElderry Books

New York   London   Toronto   Sydney   New Delhi

To C. S. Lewis, who was one of the many authors who helped shape my childhood and expand my imagination. You inspired me to write for children and check every wardrobe.—*K. W.*

For Jasmine, Salima, and Bella with love.—*A. C.*

MARGARET K. McELDERRY BOOKS
An imprint of Simon & Schuster Children's Publishing Division
1230 Avenue of the Americas, New York, New York 10020
Text copyright © 2013 by Karma Wilson
Illustrations copyright © 2013 by Anna Currey
MARGARET K. McELDERRY BOOKS is a trademark of Simon & Schuster, Inc.
For information about special discounts for bulk purchases, please contact Simon & Schuster Special Sales
at 1-866-506-1949 or business@simonandschuster.com.
The Simon & Schuster Speakers Bureau can bring authors to your live event. For more information or to book an event,
contact the Simon & Schuster Speakers Bureau at 1-866-248-3049 or visit our website at www.simonspeakers.com.
Book design by Lauren Rille
The text for this book is set in Centaur.
The illustrations for this book are rendered in pen and ink and watercolor.
Manufactured in China
0813 SCP
10 9 8 7 6 5 4 3 2 1
Library of Congress Cataloging-in-Publication Data
Wilson, Karma.
Who goes there? / Karma Wilson ; illustrated by Anna Currey. — 1st ed.
p. cm.
Summary: Just as Lewis the mouse is settling into his near-perfect home for the winter, still wondering what is missing,
he hears noises and must roar to scare away whatever horrid creature is scratching and tapping at his tree.
ISBN 978-1-4169-8002-5 (hardcover : alk. paper) — ISBN 978-1-4424-4984-8 (e-book)
[1. Mice—Fiction. 2. Noise—Fiction. 3. Fear—Fiction. 4. Dwellings—Fiction.] I. Currey, Anna, ill.
II. Title.
PZ7.W69656Who 2013
[E]—dc23
2012040994

THIS BOOK BELONGS TO

_____